101 SPOOKY BUMS

Written by Sam Harper • Illustrated by Chris Jevons

Hodder Children's Books

Spooky bum,

hooty bum,

hairy bum,

scary bum.

Slither bum,

quiver bum,

bony bum,

moany bum.

Twitchy bums, **witchy** bums,
whizzing through the sky.

Warty bums,

naughty bums -
time to say goodbye!

Goo bum,

'BOO' bum,
what a scary fright!

Howl bum, **growl** bum.
Eek! Does that one bite?

Bums in the deep dark forest,

bums in the haunted house.

Bums all playing hide-and-seek,
quiet as a mouse.

Bums in the gloomy castle,

bums in the twilight town.

Bums at the spooky disco,
dancing round and round!

This bum's rather dinky,

and this one - bleurgh, so stinky.

These bums like to trick-or-treat.
They love their spookalicious sweets!

Blizzard bum,

wizard bum, casts a fizz-whizz spell.

Fang bum,

bang! bum.

Uh-oh —
what's that smell?

And this bum's very, very,
VERY LARGE!

Bat bums,

cat bums.

This one's cute
- oh, no!

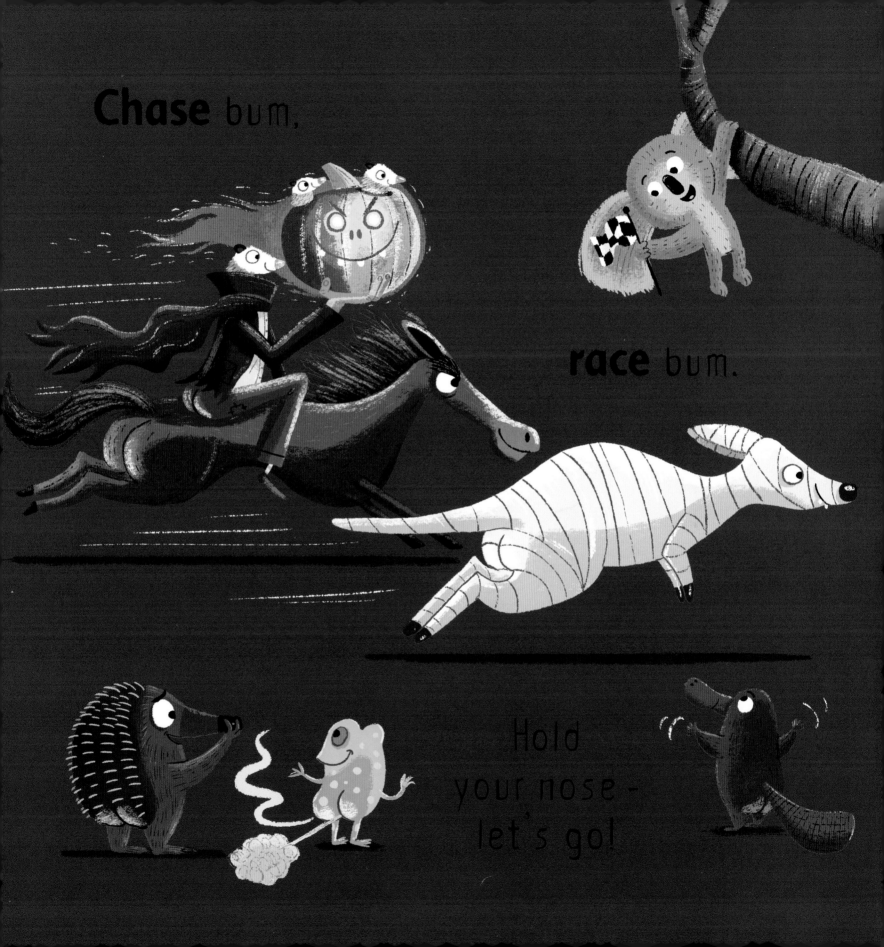

Chase bum,

race bum.

Hold
your nose -
let's go!

Sleepy bum,

creepy bum,

night bum,

fright bum.

Cool bum,

ghoul bum,

squeak bum,

shriek bum.

Tall, small, grumpy, jumpy,

terrible and **mean**.

It's time to celebrate the most
spooooooook-tacular Halloween!

There are **101** brilliant bums in this book!
How many did you spot?

For Chester
C.J.

HODDER CHILDREN'S BOOKS

First published in Great Britain in 2020
by Hodder and Stoughton

© Hachette Children's Group, 2020
Illustrations by Chris Jevons

All rights reserved

A CIP catalogue record for this book is
available from the British Library.

ISBN: 978 1 444 95668 9

1 3 5 7 9 10 8 6 4 2

Printed and bound in China

MIX
Paper from
responsible sources
FSC® C104740
FSC
www.fsc.org

Hodder Children's Books
An imprint of Hachette Children's Group
Part of Hodder and Stoughton
Carmelite House, 50 Victoria Embankment, London, EC4Y 0DZ

An Hachette UK Company
www.hachette.co.uk
www.hachettechildrens.co.uk